When a child says, 'No!' it is important to listen to and respect their voice.

This little girl knows exactly what she means when she says, 'No!'

➤ An empowering book for children of all ages! ◄

Also included:

→ 'Note to the Reader' on the importance of empowering children through discussions around rights, personal boundaries, respect, consent and choice.

→ Conversation starters and discussion questions for parents, caregivers and educators.

No Means No! was written by Jayneen Sanders — the author of the award-winning children's book on safe and unsafe touch, *Some Secrets Should Never Be Kept* and the comprehensive parents' guide, *Body Safety Education — A parents' guide to protecting kids from sexual abuse.*

www.somesecrets.info

ISBN 978-1-925089-22-6
90000
9 781925 089226

S0-AGN-940

No Means No!

Teaching children about personal boundaries, respect and consent;
empowering kids by respecting their choices and their right to say, 'No!'

by Jayneen Sanders

illustrated by Cherie Zamazing

Dedication

To my three amazing and inspiring
daughters whose voices have always been
strong and crystal clear!
Proud of you all!
J.S.

No Means No!
published by UpLoad Publishing Pty Ltd
Victoria Australia
www.upload.com.au

First published in 2015

Text copyright © Jayneen Sanders 2015
Illustration copyright © Cherie Zamazing 2015

Written by Jayneen Sanders
Illustrations by Cherie Zamazing
Designed by Ben Galpin

Cataloguing-in-Publication Data

National Library of Australia

Creator:	Sanders, Jayneen, author.
Title:	No means no! : teaching children about personal boundaries, respect and consent; empowering kids by respecting their choices and their right to say, 'no!' / Jayneen Sanders ; Cherie Zamazing.
ISBN:	9781925089226 (paperback)
Subjects:	Respect for persons. Personal space. Autonomy in children. Interpersonal relations.
Other Authors/Contributors:	Zamazing, Cherie, illustrator.
Dewey Number:	158.2

Note to the Reader

It is crucial that our children, from a very young age, are taught to have a clear, strong voice in regards to their rights — especially about their bodies. In this way, they will have the confidence to speak up when they are unhappy or feel uncomfortable in any situation. A strong, confident voice as a young child converts to a strong, confident pre-teen, teenager and adult. With the prevalence today of online and offline bullying and various forms of abuse, such as physical, emotional and sexual; our young people need to learn (from a young age) to always speak up when their rights are not being respected.

My aim in writing this book is to empower young children so they can grow up into empowered adults. When a child, teenager or adult says, 'No!' to any form of coercion, this should be immediately respected. A world where 'No!' does actually mean 'No!' can be a world with far less violence and increased respect for humankind. By educating our children to have true respect for one another, this world can be a much safer and more positive place.

Read this book with your child often. The Discussion Questions on pages 24 and 25 are important in helping you to draw out the learning for your child.

Some points to note:

→ In most cases, each character 'asks' the little girl's permission before or while engaging with her. This is important to note, as children (and teenagers and adults) should always be given the opportunity to consent or not. Just as importantly, they need to learn to ask when engaging with another person (especially as they grow into adulthood). If we force a child to show physical affection, what we are basically saying to them is that their wishes don't matter. The child should give hugs and kisses willingly, and all adults need to respect the child's choice. You may also wish to explain to people your child comes regularly into contact with, that 'manners' involve treating each other with respect and not forced and 'consent-assumed' physical contact.

→ It is important to note that adults outside the family also ask permission from children, e.g. when a child is at the dentist, the dentist should ask the child if it is okay to look inside his or her mouth. This models respect for another person's personal boundaries.

→ The scenarios in this book relate to personal space and a child's autonomy over their body. Of course, if a child is told that it's time to go to bed, or to clean their teeth, then, No Means No! is not an appropriate response. Another situation might be where a teacher or parent asks a child to hold hands with another person for safety reasons. Use the Discussion Questions on pages 24 and 25 to establish with your child when it is their right to say, 'No!' You could list these scenarios together, so the guidelines are clear for you and your child.

→ Lastly, as your child grows, provide them with choice, e.g. Would you like eggs or cereal for breakfast? What will you choose to wear today? This way your child has a say in decisions that relate directly to them. This children's book is about giving children choice, respecting their choices and personal boundaries, asking them for their consent and empowering them as they grow into adulthood .

When Auntie Jeanie asks me for a kiss,
and I don't want to ...

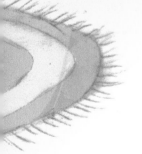

No Means No!

I can choose to blow her a kiss,
shake her hand, or give her a high five,
but if I don't want a hug or a kiss ...

No Means No!

When it's bath time and my mother asks if she can wash and dry my private parts, and I say, 'No thanks, I can do it all by myself' ...

No Means No!

I can wash and dry my own private parts today,
tomorrow or the next day because my body
is my body and I am the BOSS of it!

Sometimes my big cousin looks after me.
We run races and have fun on the swings,
but if he wants to wrestle and play tickling
games, and I don't want to ...

No Means No!

We can build a giant sandcastle in the sand or play catch with a ball, but if I don't want to wrestle or play tickling games ...

No Means No!

When someone asks to hold my hand at school and I want to walk all by myself ...

No Means No!

Sometimes, I like to walk by myself and
I don't want to hold anyone's hand.

I can say, 'No thanks'
or 'Not today',
as kindly as I can.

When people ask me things and I say, 'No' ...

I don't mean 'Maybe'
and I don't mean 'I'm not sure'.

What I REALLY mean is **No!**

So even though I may be small ...

I am strong and I have a voice that is
LOUD and **CLEAR**.

So ... when I say, 'No' ...

No Means No!

Discussion Questions for Parents, Caregivers and Educators

The following Discussion Questions are intended as a guide and can be used to initiate an open and honest dialogue with your child. Allow your child time to answer the questions and to ask some of their own. As your child grows and in daily conversations, ask them how they are feeling about a situation, what choices they wish to make and if they are okay with various activities. It is important that you value their input and listen to their voice. 'No Means No!' can be used as a teaching springboard for discussions on respect, rights, consent, personal boundaries and choice. All of these discussions only increase your child's sense of self, their confidence and empowerment.

Pages 4–5

Ask: Has anyone tried to kiss or hug you like this? How did you feel about it? What did you do? What can you do if you don't want to kiss or hug someone? *That's right! You could give them a polite and friendly high five, shake the person's hand or blow them a kiss if you know them quite well.*

Pages 6–7

Ask: Do you always have to kiss or hug a person, especially an adult? Why? Why not? (Note: It is a good idea to ask your child how they would like to greet or say goodbye to someone. By asking them and allowing them to choose, it shows that you respect their choice.) **Ask:** Do you think the little girl's parents are cross at how she is greeting Auntie Jeanie? Why not? *That's right! They understand she has the right to say, 'No!' and greet Auntie Jeanie in a way she is comfortable with. We all have an invisible personal 'bubble' around us and people need to ask permission to enter this personal space. We can choose to let them in or not.*

Pages 8–11

Ask: Where are your private parts? *Yes! They are your private body parts under your swimsuit.* (Note: Children should know the correct anatomical names for their private parts. The mouth is also a private part.) **Ask:** Do you think you are old enough to wash and dry your private parts? Why do you say that? **Say:** Remember, you are the boss of your body and if anyone touches your private parts, you can say, 'Stop!' loudly and then quickly go and tell one of the five people on your Safety Network.

(Note: Please see 'Some Secrets Should Never Be Kept' and/or 'Body Safety Education — A parents' guide to protecting kids from sexual abuse' for in-depth and comprehensive information on safe and unsafe touch, also known as Body Safety or child sexual abuse prevention education; please go to www.somesecrets.info for details).

Pages 12–15

Ask: Do you have an older brother/sister/cousin you play with? Do they listen to you when you say, 'No' to a game? What could you do if they don't listen and respect your 'No'? *Yes! You could tell a trusted adult.* **Ask:** Do you always have to do what an older person says — especially if they ask you to play a game you don't want to? *That's right! Just because the person is older doesn't mean you have to play the game.* **Say:** The older cousin in the story respected the little girl's choice and didn't play the tickling game. They both played another game instead. Remember you are the boss of your body and if you don't want to play a certain game, such as tickling or wrestling, you don't have to.

(Note: Some sexual predators will use physical games, such as tickling, wrestling and encouraging a child to ride on their back to groom the child and have them become comfortable with the physical touch. Overtime, this touch may become sexual in nature. Of course, we want our children to enjoy games that involve physical contact but the child must always be a happy and willing participant. As soon as they become uncomfortable or don't want to play that game anymore, their 'No' should be adhered to and respected, and the game should cease immediately.)

Pages 16–19

Ask: If someone wants to hold your hand or give you a hug and you don't want them to, what can you do? *That's right! You can say, 'No!' or 'I don't like that' or 'Stop!'* **Say:** Remember, you have your own invisible 'bubble' around you and if anyone comes inside your bubble, you have the right to say, 'No! I don't like that.' **Ask:** Imagine you wanted to hold someone's hand, and when you asked them they said, 'No!' What could you say and do? What if your teacher or another adult asks you to hold their hand or another child's hand when you are crossing a road — should you hold hands for your own safety? **Say:** Look at the boy. Is he worried or angry that the little girl did not want to hold is hand? *That's right! He is not worried or angry at all because he knows the little girl can make her own choices and he respects her choice not to hold his hand.* **Ask:** Why did the little girl say, 'No' in a kind way? *Yes! She did not want to hurt the boy's feelings but she still wanted to make her own choice and not hold his hand.*

Pages 20–21

Ask: What does this picture tell us about the little girl? *That's right! She is strong and important; and she is the boss of her body.* **Ask:** Can you stand like this little girl? How does it make you feel?

Pages 22–23

Say: Remember, you are the boss of your body and you have the right to say, 'No!' to any kind of touch that makes you feel uncomfortable. **Ask:** What should you do if someone touches you in a way that makes you feel unsafe? *That's right! You must get away quickly and Tell! Tell! Tell! You must keep on telling until you are believed.* **Ask:** What could you do if you saw someone else bully or not respect another person's 'No!'? *That's right! You can tell them that they have the right to say, 'No!' in a loud and clear voice. You can also tell a trusted adult.* **Ask:** Do you have any questions you would like to ask me?

About the Author

Jayneen Sanders (aka Jay Dale) is an experienced classroom teacher, the lead author for 'Engage Literacy' (published by Capstone Classroom in the US) and has authored over 100 books for children, a publisher of educational materials and the mother of three children. She is also the proud author of the children's book on safe and unsafe touch, 'Some Secrets Should Never Be Kept'. Jayneen is a passionate advocate for Body Safety Education to be taught in our schools and homes. She has written numerous blogs and articles on teaching Body Safety and has published a teaching pack to support 'Some Secrets Should Never Be Kept'.

Books by the Same Author

Some Secrets Should Never Be Kept

'Some Secrets Should Never Be Kept' is an award-winning and beautifully illustrated picture book that sensitively broaches the subject of keeping our children safe from sexual abuse. This book was written as a tool to help parents, caregivers and teachers broach the subject with children in an age-appropriate and non-threatening way. 'Some Secrets Should Never Be Kept' is now integrated into Body Safety programs throughout the United States, the United Kingdom and Australasia. It has been translated into seven languages and is published by Memory House in China.

Body Safety Education —
A parents' guide to protecting kids from sexual abuse

This essential and easy-to-read guide contains simple, practical and age-appropriate ideas on how parents and carers can protect children from sexual abuse — ensuring they grow up as assertive and confident teenagers and adults. It is crucial we empower our children through education. There is no downside to teaching children Body Safety!

For more information on these books and topics go to:
www.somesecrets.info

CPSIA information can be obtained
at www.ICGtesting.com
Printed in the USA
BVOW07s2241250516

449467BV00018B/190/P